Usborne
Phonics Readers
Toad makes a road

Phil Roxbee Cox

Illustrated by Stephen Cartwright

Edited by Jenny Tyler

Language consultant: Marlynne Grant

BSc, CertEd, MEdPsych, PhD, AFBPs, CPsychol

There is a little yellow duck to find on every page.

First published in 2006 by Usborne Publishing Ltd., Usborne House, 83-85 Saffron Hill, London EC1N 8RT, England. www.usborne.com
Copyright © 2006, 2000 Usborne Publishing Ltd.

Toad hops happily.
She has a new house on the hill.

"My new house is best," she boasts.

3

Toad waits and waits for the truck to bring her things.

Time ticks on ...

Is the truck stuck?

Toad hops down
the hill.

She's in luck.
There's the truck.

"I can't get up the hill. The load will spill."

There's no track for the truck.

So, Toad brings her things up the hill.

Toad is tired.
  With one last hop
    she flops into bed...

Next day, Toad eats toast.
"Today is my party!"

But only Billy the goat gets up the hill.

"It's far too steep, except for me or a sheep."

"What you need is a road, Toad."

"If I need a road, then I'll make a road!" says Toad.

"But toads can't make roads,"
says Billy. "That's silly."

"Wait and see!"
says Toad.

Toad clears a track.

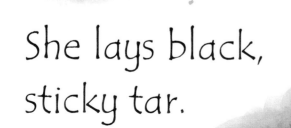

She lays black,
sticky tar.

Then she rolls it flat.

Toad's road is ready.

15

Now Toad's in luck.
Here comes the truck!

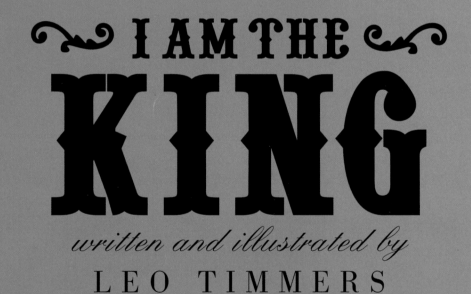

I AM THE
KING

written and illustrated by

LEO TIMMERS

'Hey, there's a crown on my back!'
squeaked Tortoise, looking round one morning.
'And it fits me to a T.'
Tortoise trotted over to show his friends.
'Look!' he cried.

'I AM THE KING!'

His friends all burst out laughing.
'You? King?' snickered Goat. 'Impossible!'
'Why's that?' said Tortoise.

'Because you're much too slow,
that's why. Besides, a real king has
a long white beard, like me.
See, the crown fits me perfectly.'

'I AM THE KING!'

'Don't make me laugh,' spluttered Flamingo.
'That's a hairy chin, not a beard!
Style's the thing for a king.
The crown suits me splendidly!'

'I AM THE KING!'

'Feather-brain,' hissed Snake.

'A king must be especially smart.

'Watch while I do something special with this crown.

Doesn't it sit superbly on me?'

'I AM THE KING!'

'Nonsense!' grunted Pig.
'A good king is deliciously round.
I know where to put this crown.
Look, we're made for each other.'

'I AM THE KING!'

'What a joke!' cried Crocodile.
'Who needs a roly-poly pig for a king,
try a tough-talking Croc instead.
Give me the crown!
See, it's just my size!'

'I AM THE KING!'

'Listen friends.' Elephant spoke.
'Don't get angry, but not one of you is king material. A king is old and wise and grey and this crown fits me like a glove.
Mmm, do I feel kingly.'

'I AM THE KING!'

'Yee haa!' screeched Ape.
'My kind of king plays pranks, like me.
Bye! The crown is mine!'
Ape ran off, shrieking,

'I AM THE KING!'

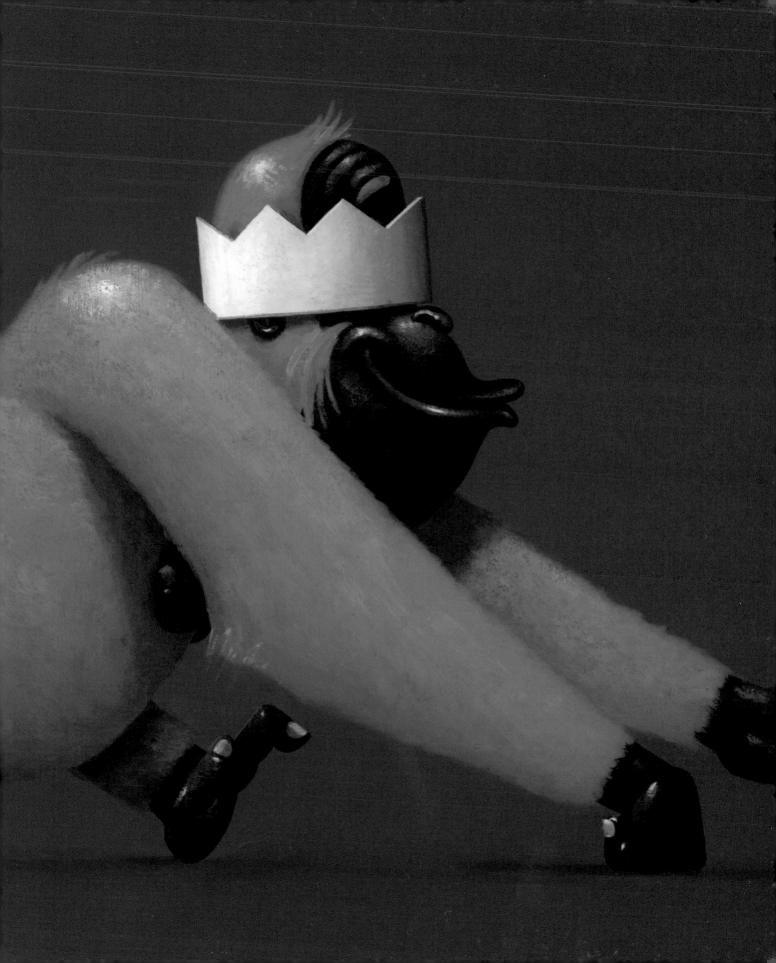

'Catch the thief!' trumpeted Elephant.

'Wait till I get hold of you,' snapped Crocodile.

'Stand still!' snorted Pig.

'Stop!' hissed Snake.

'Give it back!' flapped Flamingo.

'My crown!' bleated Goat.

'It's not fair!' Tortoise sniffed.

Ape ran so fast, he couldn't stop. Crash!
Everything went quiet. Very quiet.
'Lion . . .' someone whispered at last.

Without a word, Lion placed
the crown solemnly on his head.
Ape was amazed. 'It fits him perfectly.'
'So it does!' they all agreed.

'LION IS THE KING!
LONG LIVE THE KING!'

This edition published in 2007 by
Gecko Press, PO Box 9335, Marion Square
Wellington 6141, New Zealand
info@geckopress.com
Translation by Bill Nagelkerke
English translation © Gecko Press 2007

Cataloguing-in-Publication data for this title is available from the
National Library of New Zealand

First published in Belgium by Clavis Uitgeverij, Amsterdam-Hasselt 2006
Text and illustrations © Clavis Uitgeverij, Amsterdam-Hasselt 2006
All rights reserved
Original title: *Ik ben de koning!*

Typeset by Archetype, Wellington
Printed in Italy

Hardback ISBN 978-0-9582787-4-4
Paperback ISBN 978-0-9582787-2-0

Also by Leo Timmers: *Who's Driving?* (GECKO PRESS 2006)

For more curiously good books visit www.geckopress.com